Sam's Bush Journey

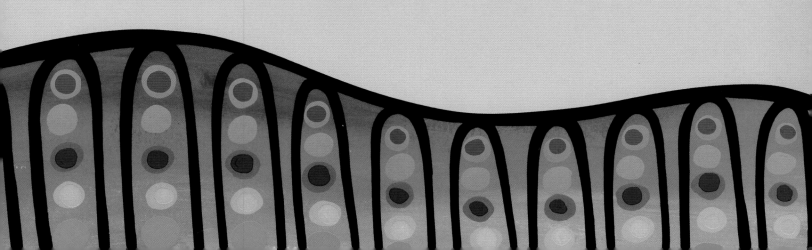

For the children of the bush–SM and EK
To my Uncle Pat, who knows about the bush,
teaches me and takes me on amazing journeys–BB

Little Hare Books
8/21 Mary Street, Surry Hills
NSW 2010 AUSTRALIA

www.littleharebooks.com

Copyright © text Sally Morgan and Ezekiel Kwaymullina 2009
Copyright © illustrations Bronwyn Bancroft 2009

First published 2009

National Library of Australia
Cataloguing-in-Publication entry

Morgan, Sally, 1951-
Sam's Bush Journey / Sally Morgan, Ezekiel Kwaymullina ; illustrator, Bronwyn Bancroft.
9781921541049 (hbk.)
For primary school age.
Kwaymullina, Ezekiel. Bancroft, Bronwyn.
A823.3

Designed by Vida & Luke Kelly
Produced by Pica Digital, Singapore
Printed in China through Phoenix Offset

5 4 3 2 1

Sam's Bush Journey

Sally Morgan and Ezekiel Kwaymullina
Illustrated by Bronwyn Bancroft

LITTLE HARE
www.littleharebooks.com

Sam loved staying with his nanna, except for one thing. Her house was surrounded by bush.

Nanna liked to take Sam for long walks. But when they got home, Sam's legs and arms would be covered in scratches from the spiky shrubs that grew in the bush.

Nanna liked to walk deep into the gum forest. But the gum trees shed their leaves and bark, and sometimes they shed their branches too.

Sam was afraid that a branch would fall on his head.

Nanna liked to feed the birds at the waterhole near her house, but it buzzed with mosquitoes.

Sam always ended up with itchy red bites that he scratched even in his sleep.

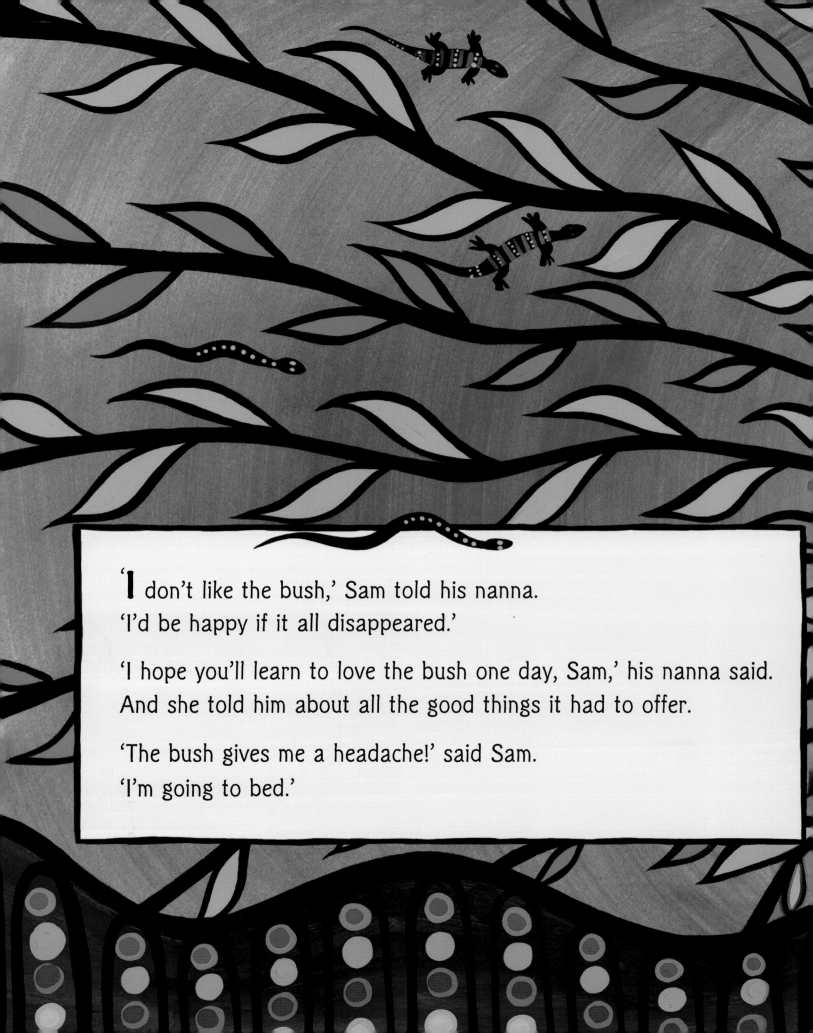

'I don't like the bush,' Sam told his nanna.
'I'd be happy if it all disappeared.'

'I hope you'll learn to love the bush one day, Sam,' his nanna said.
And she told him about all the good things it had to offer.

'The bush gives me a headache!' said Sam.
'I'm going to bed.'

When Sam next opened his eyes, he wasn't in his soft, comfortable bed. He was in the bush!

He was tired and hungry, he was surrounded by spiky shrubs and he had no idea how to get home.

Then Sam heard his nanna calling him, and he headed toward the sound of her voice.

Sam walked and walked. The further he walked, the more his stomach grumbled.

Then he remembered what his nanna had told him.

There's plenty of food in the bush.

When he looked closer at the shrubs he saw they were loaded with berries. Sam had never eaten berries before, but his nanna had told him which ones to pick.

The berries were juicy and delicious.

Sam's stomach soon stopped grumbling.

Sam kept walking.

The sky grew dark and stormy. Thunder rumbled. Lightning flashed. Rain poured down. Sam was shivering and soaking wet.

Then he remembered something else his nanna had told him.

There's plenty of shelter in the bush.

He saw an old gum tree. It was tall and wide, with a hollow in its trunk.

Sam climbed inside. It was warm and dry and smelt of eucalyptus.

By the time the rain had passed, Sam had stopped shivering.

The clouds soon disappeared and Sam kept walking. The sun came out. It shone hot and strong.

Sam began to sweat. His hair stuck to his head. His mouth was parched and his throat hurt.

Then he remembered something else his nanna had told him.

There's fresh water in the waterhole.

But Sam didn't know where to find the waterhole.

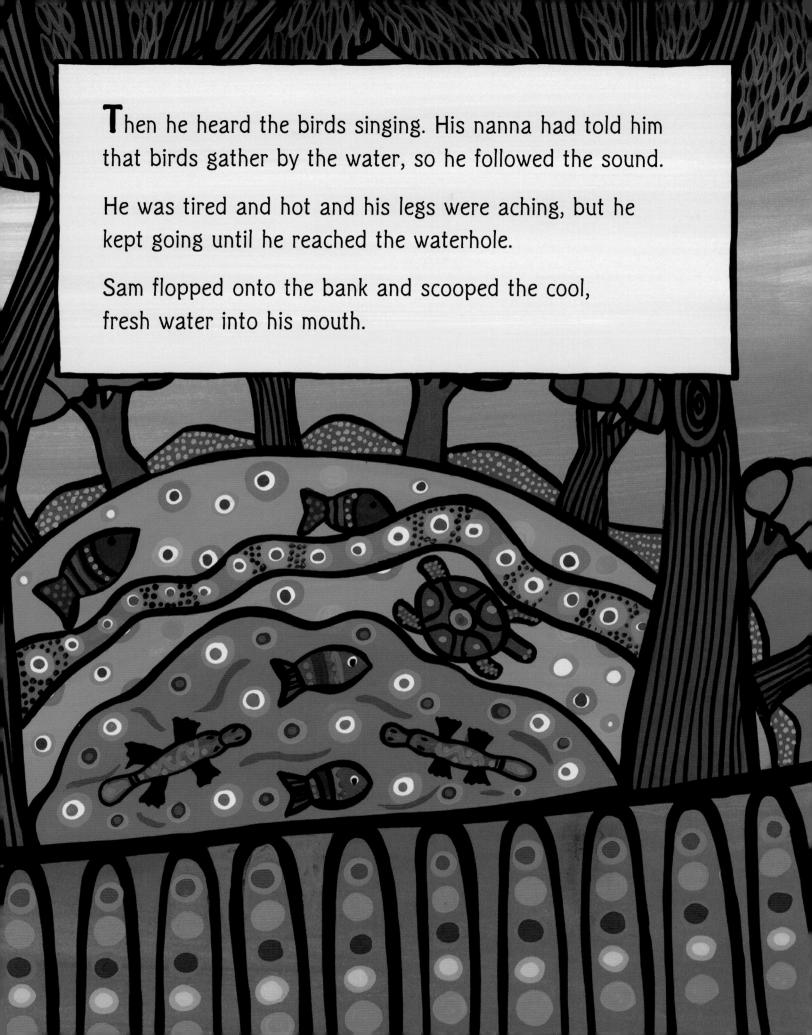

Then he heard the birds singing. His nanna had told him that birds gather by the water, so he followed the sound.

He was tired and hot and his legs were aching, but he kept going until he reached the waterhole.

Sam flopped onto the bank and scooped the cool, fresh water into his mouth.

Sam was worn out.

He curled up in the shade of a tree and closed his eyes.

When he opened them again, he wasn't in the bush. He was in his soft, comfortable bed.

'**B**reakfast time!' Nanna called out from the kitchen.

Sam felt like he'd been walking all night, and he ate a huge breakfast.

'I'm going to visit the waterhole,' said his nanna after breakfast. 'But you can stay here if it gives you a headache.'

'Oh no!' replied Sam. 'I'd like to come!'

The birds at the waterhole made a racket as Sam and Nanna arrived.

'Why, Sam,' Nanna laughed, 'if I didn't know better, I'd think they were saying good morning to you.'

'Maybe they are, Nanna,' Sam smiled. 'Maybe they are.'

SALLY MORGAN is a Palkyu person from the Pilbara in the north-west of Western Australia. She was born in Perth in 1951 and works at the School of Indigenous Studies at the University of Western Australia.

Sally is an artist and a writer and is well known for her award-winning book *My Place*, which documents the journey of her family back to their people and their country. Sally has also written a number of books for children, the most recent being the *Curly and the Fent* series, which she co-authored with her children. Sally is an ambassdor of Indigenous Literacy Day.

EZEKIEL KWAYMULLINA is a Palkyu person from the Pilbara in the north-west of Western Australia. He was born in Perth in 1983 and works full-time on his writing. Ezekiel is a co-author of the *Curly and the Fent* series and is currently working on a fantasy novel for young adults.

BRONWYN BANCROFT was born in Tenterfield, northern New South Wales. Her father, Bill, was Bundjalung, Djanbun clan and her mother, Dorothy, is of Scottish and Polish descent. As well as being a children's illustrator, Bronwyn is a leading Australian artist and works in many different mediums.

Bronwyn has illustrated several award-winning books for children. Her most recent books with Little Hare have been the highly acclaimed *Possum and Wattle: My Big Book of Australian Words* (a 2008 Children's Book Council of Australia Notable Book), *Malu Kangaroo* (by Judith Morecroft), *An Australian 1,2,3 of Animals* and *An Australian abc of Animals*. Her most recent publication is *W is for Wombat: My First Australian Word Book.* She received the May Gibbs Fellowship from the Dromkeen Centre for Children's Literature in 2000.

[9]